D1154516

# A SONG SO BLACK, SO PROUD!

R.J. OWENS AND ILLUSTRATED BY KEISHA OKAFOR

PUBLISHED BY SLEEPING BEAR PRESS™

I'm the Black is Beautiful movement,
just oozing with pride.

I've been flowing strong since I was born
in
1968

Like the Mississippi River
running up and down the States.

I'M A SONG SO BLACK, SO PROUD.

SING IT STRONG! SING IT LOUD!

I'm a bass-bumping
drum-thumping
chunky funk machine.

I'm the King of Soul
hyped up on the song that he sings.

I'M A SONG
SO BLACK,
SO PROUD.

SING IT
STRONG!

SING IT
LOUD!

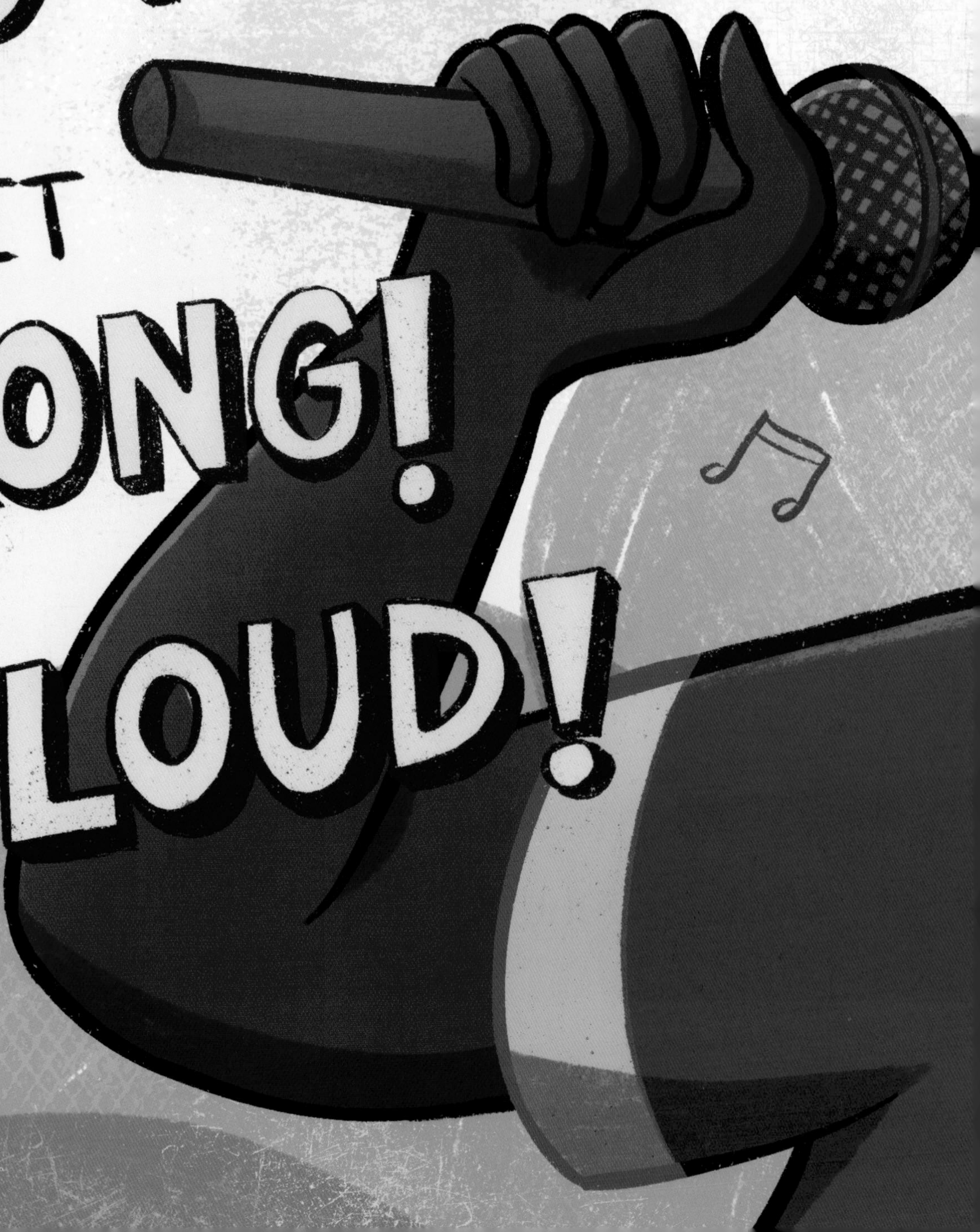

I'm a black-gloved sprinter
lifting gold up to the sky.

I'm a rock 'n' roll inventor
with the volume turned up high.

I've got boots on the pavement
stepping up, standing out.

Lift up every voice and shout
is what I'm all about.

I'm a so BLACK, SING IT SING I

Song so PROUD. STRONG! LOUD!

I'm a soul-blooded, bold-plated roller-coaster ride.

Through the past, present, future, peaks and dips, side by side.

I'm free to inhale, exhale,
take a breath, breathe.

Free to take a stand
on two feet or one knee.

Free to march in the streets
to the boom BAM beats.

Stirring up good trouble
for a vote or a seat.

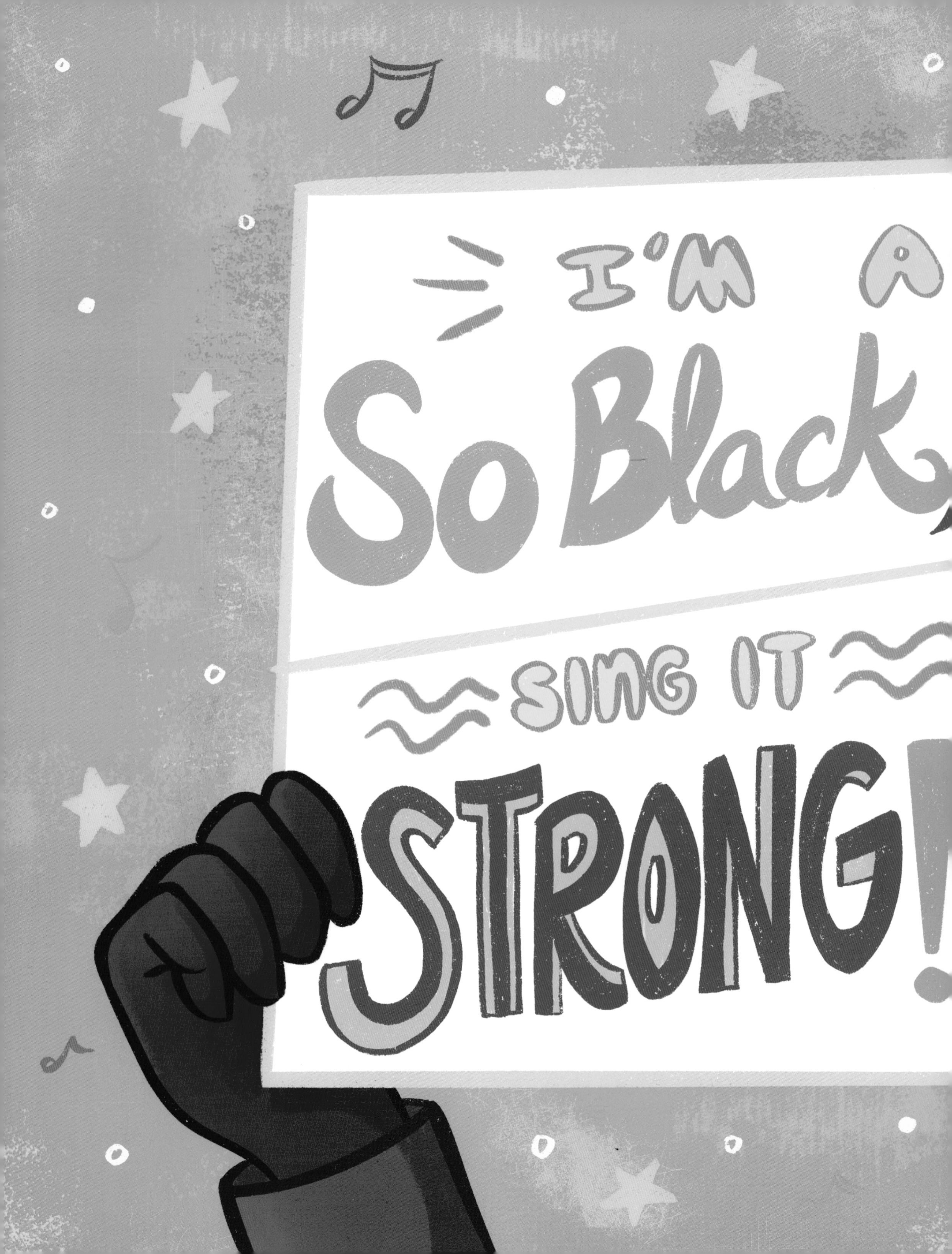
I'M A
So Black,
SING IT
STRONG!

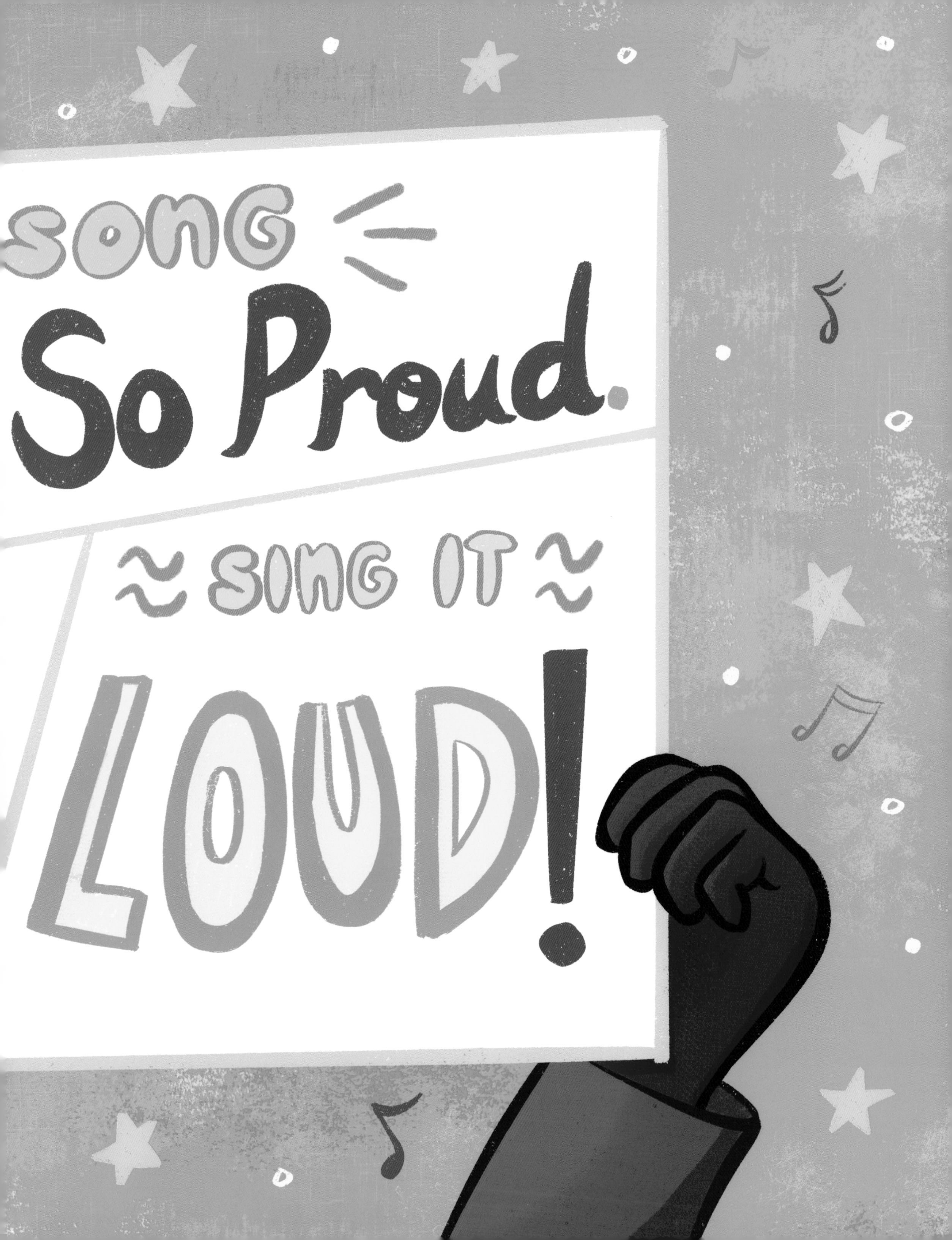
SONG
So Proud.
SING IT
LOUD!

I waft around like hickory smoke
at backyard barbecues.
I'm topping charts on Spotify,
I'm on the evening news.

I'm tumbling out of Usher's mouth
and rolling with the times.
I'm getting up, getting involved,
and moving your behind.

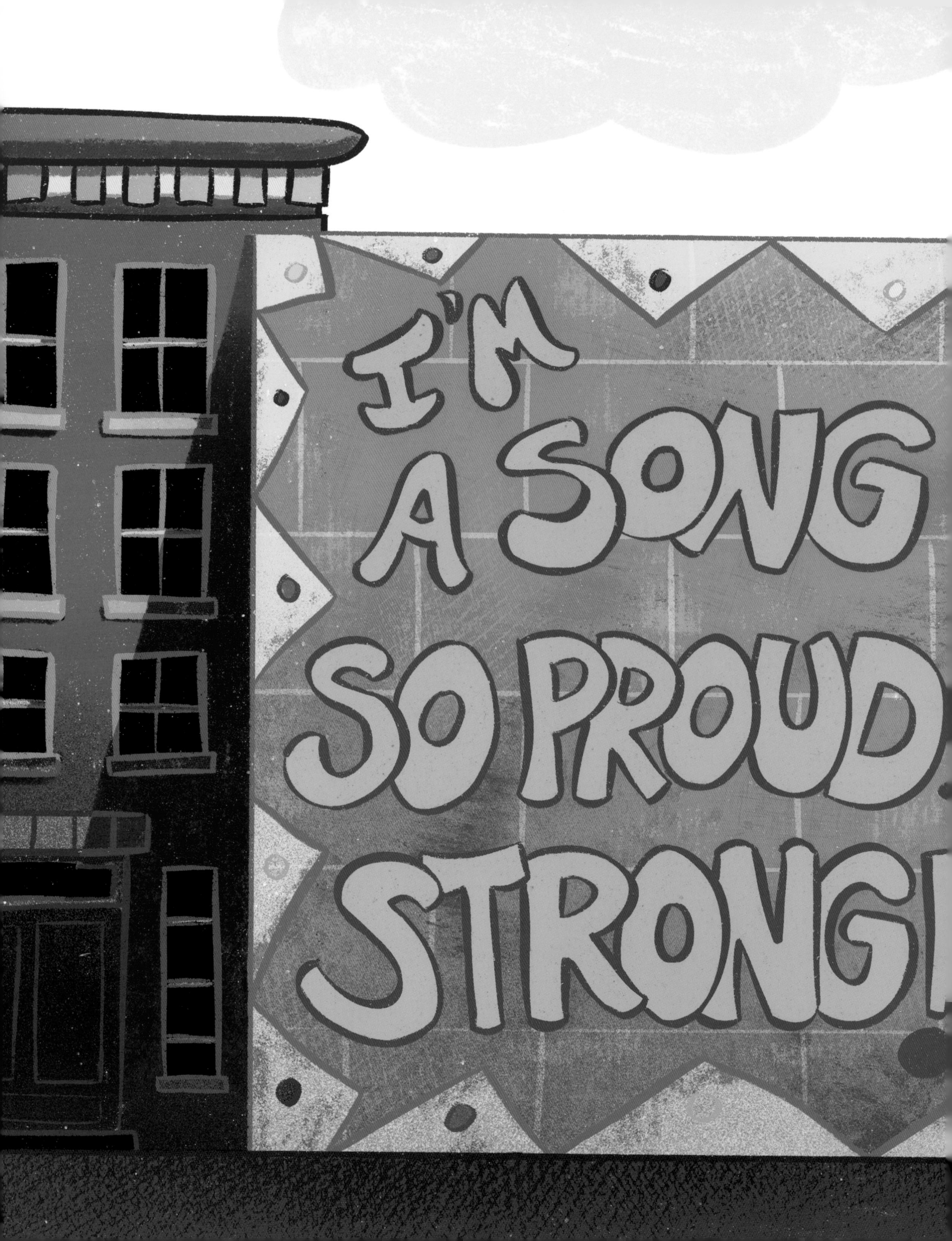
I'M
A SONG
SO PROUD
STRONG!

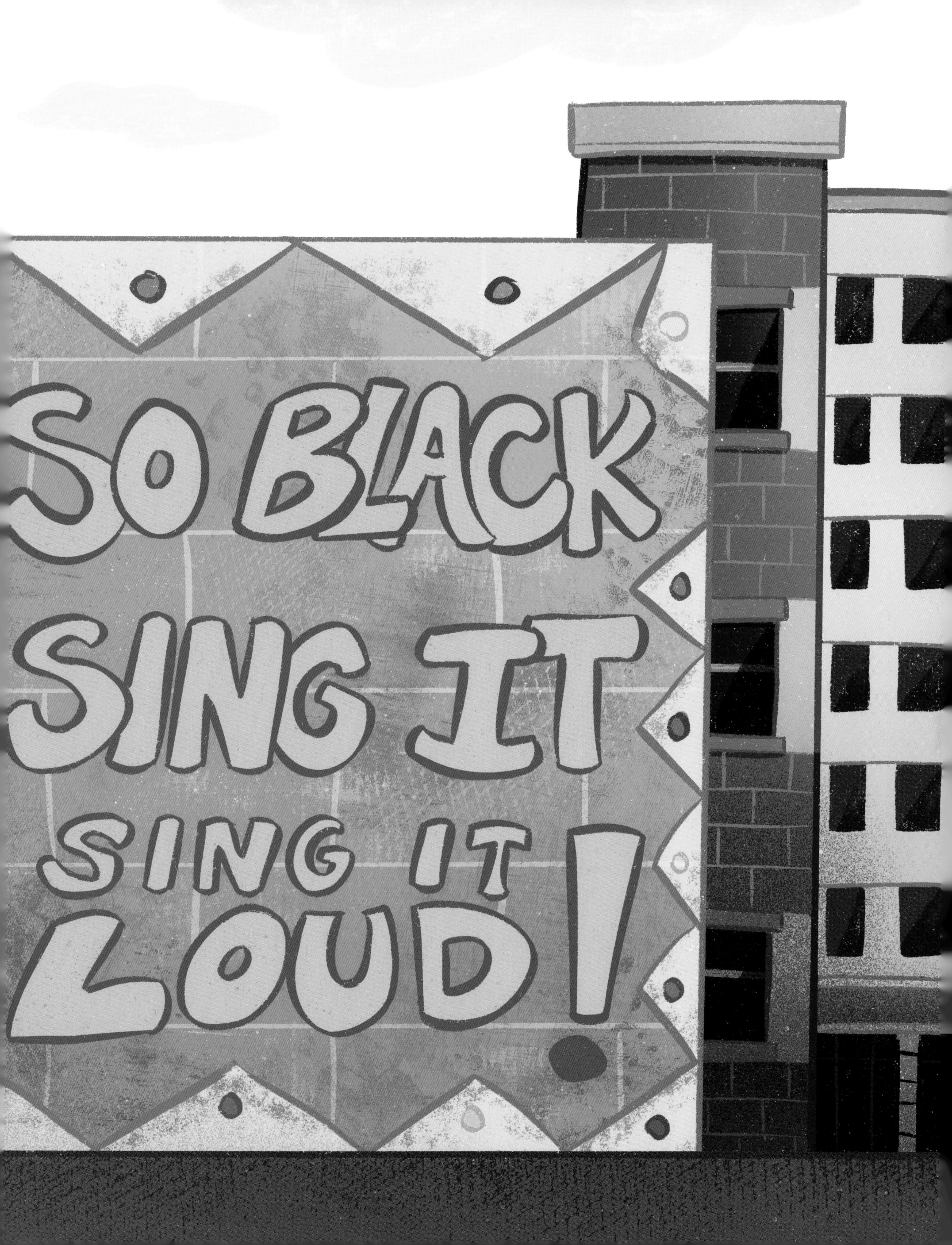
SO BLACK
SING IT
SING IT
LOUD!

I'm a mountaineer for justice
in the quest for reckoning.

Topping off the mountaintop
with red, black, and green.

I'm a supersonic beacon
shining light, glowing Black.

An auditory architect,
a blueprint for rap.

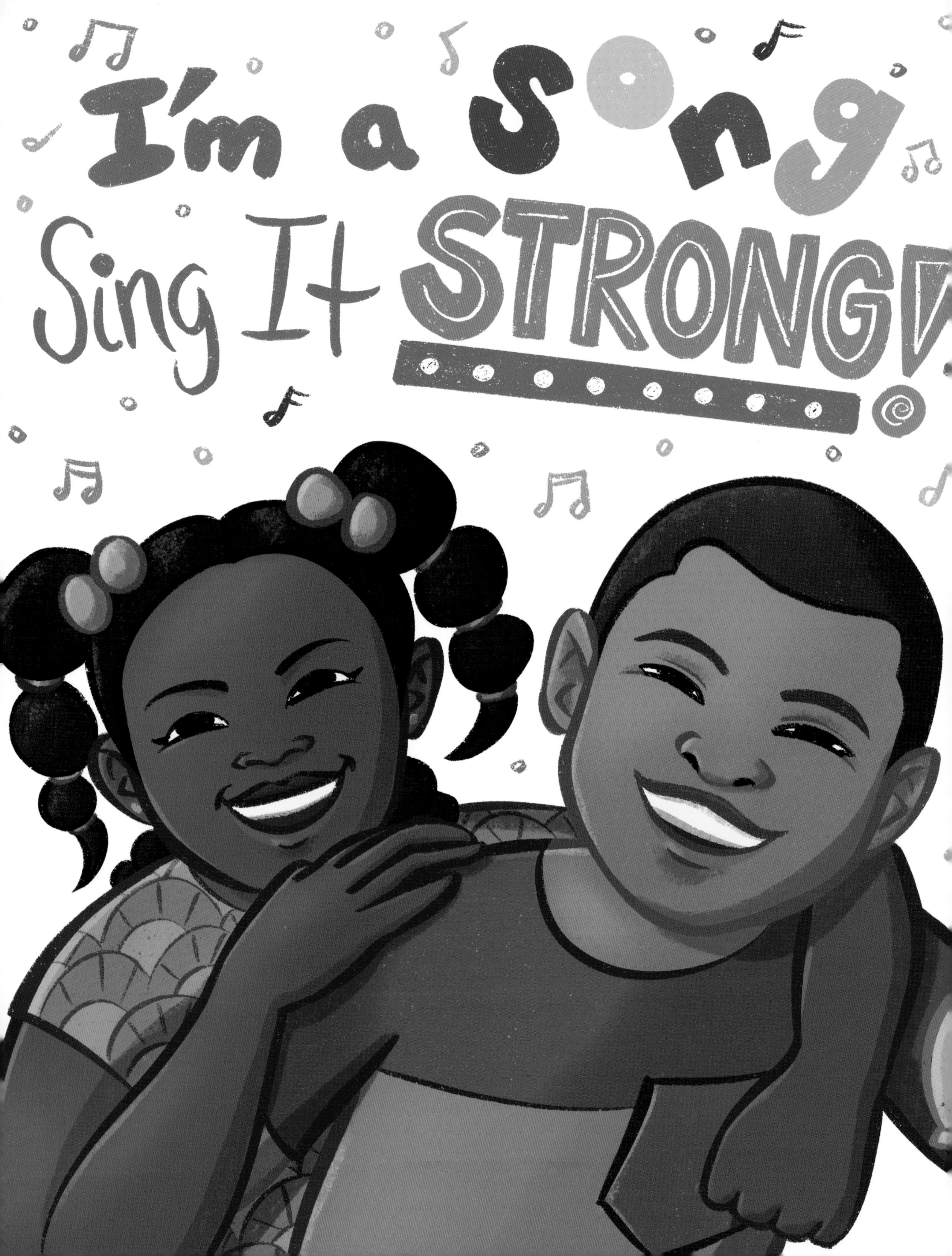
I'm a Song
Sing It STRONG!

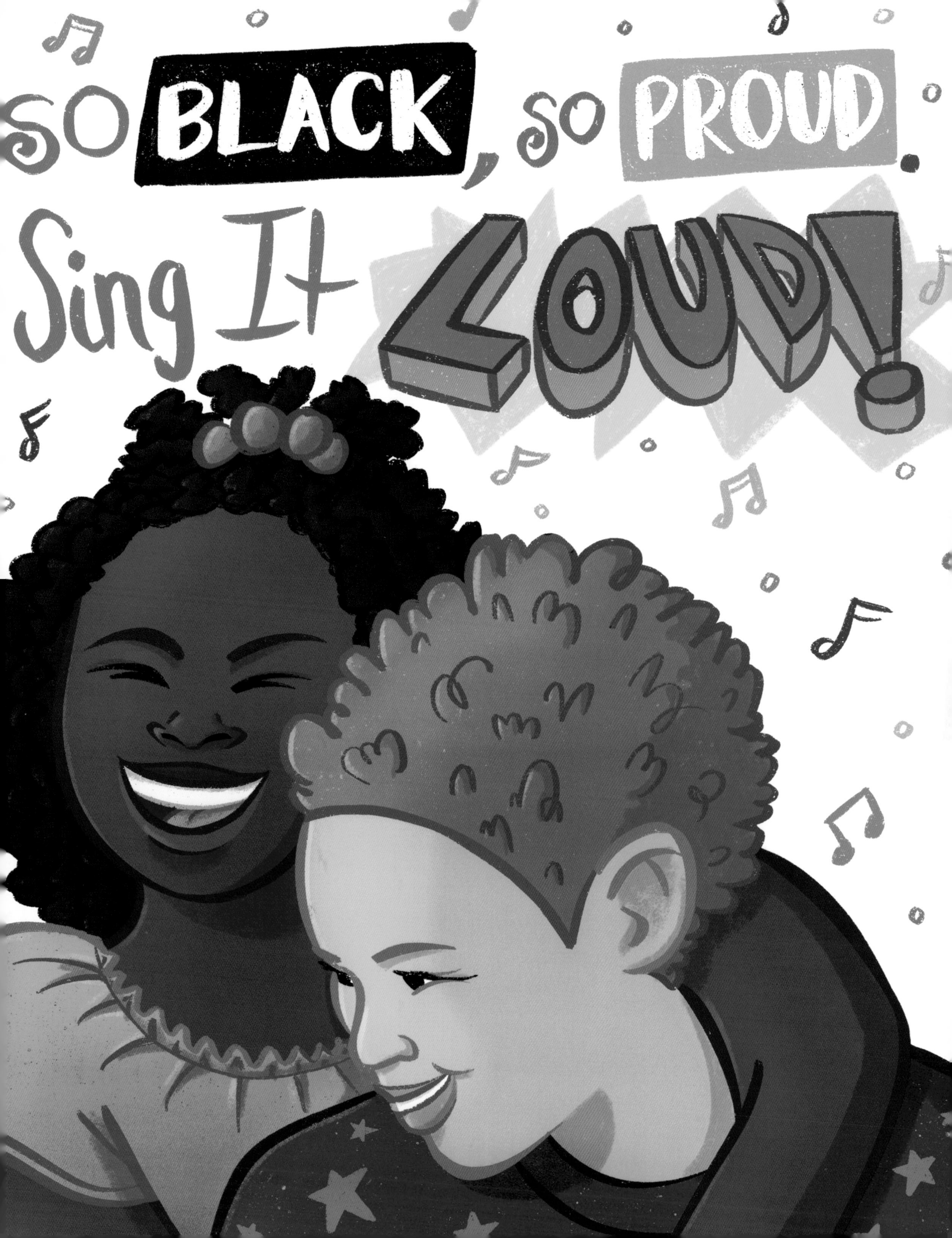
SO BLACK, SO PROUD.
Sing It LOUD!

I'm a moonlit midnight panther
with a glide in my stride.

I'm busting up the darkness
like the sun on the rise.

I'm in your face,
Momma's face,
Daddy's face too.

I'm Papa's face
when Grandma does
the camel walk
with you.

I'm BLACK Life Magic
1619
to the present,
flexing majestic presence.

1619

And I just keep rocking on,
hear the call of the horns
from up north to down home.

I'm BLACK Life Forever,
don't know the meaning of never,
excel at any endeavor.

And you've been hearing my song
since the day you were born—
I won't leave you alone.

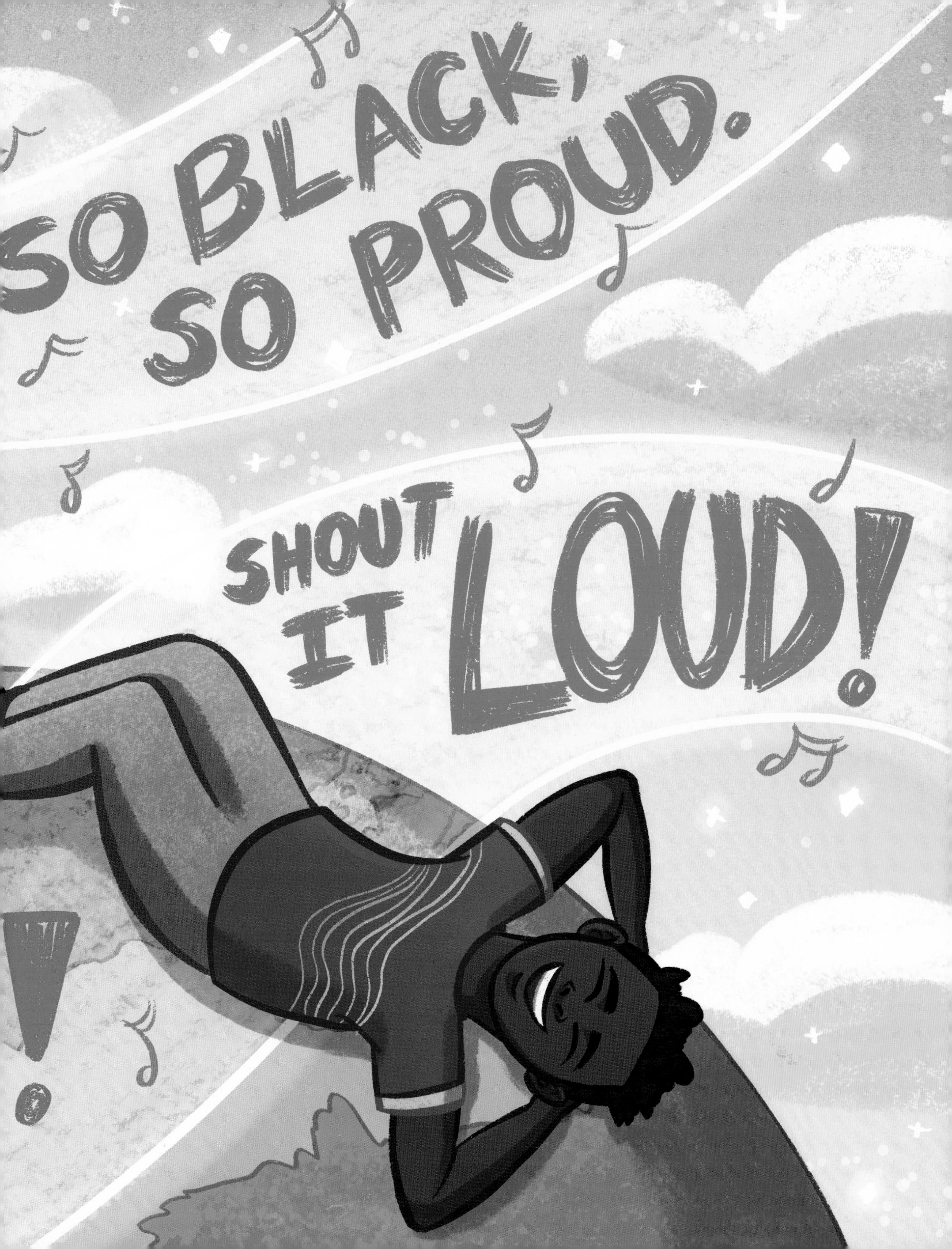
SO BLACK, SO PROUD.
SHOUT IT LOUD!

# "Say It Loud—I'm Black and I'm Proud" A Song Speaks for Itself

I was born on a napkin in a Los Angeles hotel room.

James Brown jotted down just a few words at first, scratched out with a ballpoint pen. But by the time we hit the Vox Recording Studio on August 7, 1968, well, I don't have to tell you.

I was on my way to My Bad Self.

Mr. Brown wanted to make a song to inspire self-love, self-pride, *Black* pride. And togetherness—no fighting one another over nothing.

He wanted to reach kids with this message of pride and unity, so he recruited kids to chant my chorus, to make the song sound like a song for kids.

They tell me that the kids came straight out of a Los Angeles neighborhood near the recording studio. Kids of all different races, all miked up, singing the song's refrain.

The radio stations didn't want to play me at first.

James had to take out full-page ads, urging listeners to turn the stations off unless they turned me on. The message came through loud and clear: When the man known as the Godfather of Soul rapped, people's eyes popped open.

Radio came to its senses and put the needle on the record.

After that, you couldn't walk down the street without hearing me thundering out of woofers and tweeters all around planet Earth. You couldn't camel walk without hearing me either. That's a dance, you know. Kind of like the moonwalk, only, well, camel.

I went on to blow up the Billboard Hot 100 and become an anthem for the civil rights movement and a mover and shaker for the Black is Beautiful movement. That's when Negro became Black and Black looked itself in the mirror and said, "Hello, Beautiful."

And you won't believe this: I even performed onstage live at the inauguration of President Richard Milhous Nixon in 1969. Told you so.

You already know rappers love to sample me. If you don't know, ask Eric B. & Rakim and LL Cool J and on and on till the sun breaks dawn, and you just don't stop.

And yep, I'm still going strong. Look, there's Usher, gleaming and beaming my lyrics at the opening of the National Museum of African American History. And there I am on Spotify, still the one, number one, far, far from done.

Right on, DJ, go ahead and put me on the turntable. And never, ever hesitate to

Sing A SONG so BLACK, so PROUD. SING IT STRONG! SING IT LOUD!

# Author's Note

"Say It Loud—I'm Black and I'm Proud," written and performed by James Brown, was released in 1968, four months after the assassination of Dr. Martin Luther King Jr. The song was a wake-up call, a call to action, and a call to look in the mirror, all rolled up into one. It made you feel like you *were* somebody who mattered. It made you feel confident to walk with your head held up a little higher. It made you feel like not only was it okay to be Black, it was the only thing you ever wanted to be. You grew out your Afro as a badge of honor. You said *Hey, brother* and *Hey, sister* to people you passed on the street. You stood up to the world and said, *This is me, and I'm all right.* You said, *Yes, I'm Black* and *Yes, I'm proud.* And yes, without a drop of doubt, you said it loud.

## Timeline

**1619**

The Soul of America arrives from Africa

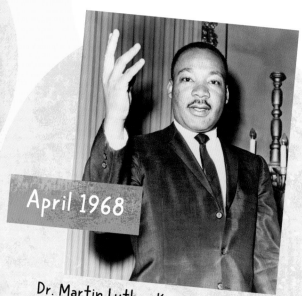

**April 1968**

Dr. Martin Luther King Jr. assassinated

**August 1968**

"Say It Loud" released: James Brown abandons "conk" (straightened hair) for Afro

**October 1968**

Sprinters Tommie Smith and John Carlos raise gloved fists during medal ceremony at Olympic Games in Mexico City

**June 1970**

Marchers chant "Say it loud, gay is proud!" at the first gay pride parade, the Stonewall Uprising in New York City

**September 2016**

Usher sings "Say It Loud" at the opening concert for Smithsonian National Museum of African American History and Culture in Washington, D.C.

**May 2020**

George Floyd protests begin

**June 2020**

"Say It Loud" is number one on Spotify's Black Lives Matter playlist

**Further Reading:**

"Black is Beautiful: The Emergence of Black Culture and Identity in the 60s and 70s." Blog post available online at the National Museum of African American History & Culture, Smithsonian.

*James Brown: Black and Proud* / Xavier Fauthoux; translated by Jeremy Melloul and Edward Gauvin, San Diego: IDW, 2019

*I Feel Good: A Memoir of a Life of Soul* / James Brown New York: New American Library, 2005

*The One: The Life and Music of James Brown* / RJ Smith New York: Gotham Books, 2012

*For Ruth Owens and James Owens,*
*so strong, so proud, so majestic in their presence*
*—RJ*


*To all of the Black children who picked up this book,*
*may you celebrate and be proud of the skin you're in*
*—Keisha*

## SLEEPING BEAR PRESS™

Text Copyright © 2023 R.J. Owens
Illustration Copyright © 2023 Keisha Okafor
Design Copyright © 2023 Sleeping Bear Press
All rights reserved.
No part of this book may be reproduced in any manner
without the express written consent of the publisher,
except in the case of brief excerpts in critical reviews
and articles. All inquiries should be addressed to:
Sleeping Bear Press
2395 South Huron Parkway, Suite 200
Ann Arbor, MI 48104
www.sleepingbearpress.com © Sleeping Bear Press

Printed and bound in China.
10 9 8 7 6 5 4 3 2 1

Library of Congress Cataloging-in-Publication Data on File.
ISBN 978-1-53411-270-4 (hardcover)

**Timeline Photo Credits:**
1619: Slave ships on the ocean. Wood engraving by Smyth. Wellcome Images V0041266.jpg
April 1968: Library of Congress, Demarsico, Dick, photographer. Dr. Martin Luther King, Jr., half-length portrait, facing front / World Telegram & Sun photo by Dick DeMarsico. , 1964. Photograph. https://www.loc.gov/item/00651714/.
August 1968: © Ken Hawkins / Alamy Stock Photo
October 1968: Angelo Cozzi, "Tommie Smith and John Carlos at the 1968 Mexican Olympic Games," Mondadori Publishers, October 16, 1968, http://bit.ly/22xcKkg (accessed November 25, 2015)
June 1970: Jean-Nickolaus Tretter Collection in GLBT Studies, University of Minnesota Libraries, Minneapolis. Author Jim Chalgren
September 2016: GiuseppeCrimeni / Shutterstock.com
May 2020: XanderGallery / Shutterstock.com
June 2020: Kraft74 / Shutterstock.com